C000072043

Meet Me at The Causeway

A compilation of Bardic tasks (and other original works)
submitted by Mozinah for assessment by her mentor for
druidic grading by Steve Tatler, of which she was
awarded the highest grade of Oak.

Mozinah the Seer

Roswell
Publishing

Meet Me at The Causeway
The Introduction

Her whole world was constantly shattered into a million pieces of sparkling glass with every waking moment she was away from her home.

He was in a permanent state of isolation always running from his fate, too feared to see anything else other than all he knew.

And on one day, their worlds unknowingly collided, and nothing was ever the same again. Even though neither of them knew it, nothing was ever the same. No matter how they pushed and pulled to be away, like magnets they kept finding each other. Each person allowing the other to dream a little more than they are used to doing so, believing everything is possible and not once ever acting on those possibilities.

Their story is for you to decide.

As the waves unpredictably crash against the monolithic causeway stones in a poetic manner, or the light hits the old castle walls in a glimmer of a hope, here are two people who will never have their answers. They are not star-crossed lovers, they are not friends, and they are not enemies.

Yet, when he sees the full moon he is reminded of her glow, and when he feels the sun on his back he feels her strength. She is everywhere he looks.

Who are they? What is their purpose? Why do they matter?

That is for you to decide. And one day, their story will be told, when they are old, oh so very old.

There's a land I had to find,
A land I knew was mine.
There's a land I knew I'd see,
A land that feels like part of me.
Where fields so green,
Meet sea so blue,
The mountains spoke,
As Lugh shone through.
A land so alive,
It awakened me,
For the first time, I could clearly see.
I had remembered the land,
It never forgot me.
I heard the sea, in my sleep,
Saw the cliffs, in my dreams,
It was always a part of me.

I think of you when the sun rises on a land I've yet to
fully roam,
When the moon is full and laying low.
I think of you when certain sounds echo in my ear.
I think of you,
because you were once here.
You're everywhere and you know it,
A voice in a town you're not native.
Driving me away, driving me far,
All I hear is the distant hum of guitar.
Took myself for a coffee to block you from my thoughts,
It didn't work.
You're still breathing, I can feel it, don't know why it
means anything.
I think you're my past life,
I don't want to revisit.

Take me to the forests so tall and bold,
I don't care if the wolves are prowling.
I can feel the heat of energy,
As our hearts stand howling.
Take me to the trees,
I want to see the sun set behind the pines.
Whisper to me as you lay me on the grass,
That you'll always be mine, tenderly.

In my dreams I see the sea so vividly, so peacefully.
Sunsets cast a faint glow over the moody blue causeway
stones,
I hear the lovers nearby at the red rock mountainside,
Running high to hide for the safety of their lives.
I hear uncertain heartbeats and wonder if they're the
same as mine.
Do I stay? Do I run?
Do I dare find what I'm looking for?
Deep in the heart of Antrim
Deep in the heart of my beloved Antrim
Where my love waits
Crashing against the tides.

A Deeper Peace

Ask the trees for a deeper peace and they will serenade
you gently as the wind runs through their leaves, like a
loving hand caressing the hair on your head when you
feel weak.
Ask the sun for a sign and you will get a brighter day,
like the dreams of far away places that fill with you hope
and keep you alive.
Ask the moon for healing and you will be gifted the
softest auric kiss, as though the love of one who has
passed is right there with you again.
Ask the stars for a message you are yet to find, and they
will leave a trail like a bottle at sea, landing at your feet
unknowingly.
Oh gods, oh universe, whoever you are, take me home to
find my deeper peace.
I have felt it before I am sure. In my mind that does not
stop, I felt peace once.
As I walked the edge of the land, the castle sits on the
cliffside, strong yet aware of its pending eventual death,
I felt free.
I longed for the sun to never let me go there and then. I
begged the sea to never forget the sound of my voice and
I spoke to the mountains as they whispered tales of
lovers on the run, chasing their dreams and running
purely on their hearts desires to be together.
I sit at the side of the sea, where the rocks gather in
strange shapes and the boulders are large enough to sit
on. I felt my heart beating, all of my senses awakened,
my mind clear.
I did not think, I was simply 'being'.
I asked the waves to wash away my hurts and clear my
soul.
Never, has anywhere, felt more alive than here.
I could see in my minds eye the ancestors of the past. I

could smell their fires burning, the rituals of the past lingered in the air like a never ending swirl of magic. Before I left, I placed my hands on the mountainside, and whispered 'If I am meant to be here, bring me back, don't let me go'.

And now, back and forth I go, to be with my deeper peace.

As the bards do, I daydream and ponder at the
landscapes before me, romantically.
I hear songs and think of you as the words dance around
my mind and enter my heart of maybes.
Do you feel me when the sun rays beat down on a day
that was otherwise dark?
Do you?
Can't you understand the break in the clouds is my need
for you.
The passion inside burns so deeply, and as the melody
swims in my soul I want nothing more than to kiss you.
I want to run my fingers through your hair and grab the
locks with desperation only two lovers understand,
barely taking a breath in between each moment.
My body longs for you, my heart aches at every fragile
whisper, between kisses, of needing more and more of
you.
I need you as though you are oxygen, and with you I rely
on my last breath being as full as the midsummer sun.

She disappeared through the clouds,
Reminding me of all I had left behind.
Patchwork fields of green are woven tightly together,
Memories of a summer I never had,
Come flooding back.
Memories of a life that was once mine,
Returning to claim every last breath,
Of every word I ever said.

Consumption

Next lifetime, I wish to fall in love with you again.
Only, the green fields will be ours and not just mine, and
the trees you love will not be just yours.
There will be no time,
Only love and sunsets
And the land will be ours to roam free in, forever.
I am desperate to fall in love with you,
Where the skies are a new blue on a good day so true
We will dance under the sun and light of Lugh.
Our hearts will beat with the movement of our limbs,
Climbing rapidly as lovers we run to the mountains,
Nestled in caves as the elements collide, waves crashing
on the evening tide we stay alive.
I make a truce to the gods to be good this life, in
exchange for an embrace, under Dunluce skies.
In our next cycle,
There will be no time, no set days.
Only our love and sunsets at causeway.
The druids dare not even question our love,
For it supersedes their powers gifted from gods above.
It is stronger than the world's only they know and with
their blessing we go, we go.
We go forwards, never looking back.
I am desperate to fall in love with you.
I am so, very, desperate.
It consumes me.

My Premonition

When all is said and done
My life well lived and loved,
When I've nothing left anymore
Wise at 84.
I shall sit watching the suns tones of warmth and glow,
At my castle.
There I will hold a photo of us,
Remember our life,
I will breathe in the air one last time,
And close my eyes.
Returning to you my love,
Where we can both fly over the sunrise.

Meet me at the causeway, not because I am asking,
But because you know I will be there, breathing in the
same air,
My ancestors once shared.
They're your family too, and everyone we know,
Here are we are, alone with no walls,
And only mythology between us.
Meet me at the causeway, I can tell from your heartbeat
you want to,
Gaze in the waves that are as dark as Omagh skies as we
observe the same setting sun.
Maybe we will never need anything more than this,

to say all we have to say.

Those five words can heal us,
Meet me at the causeway.

Ocean

You'll always be the sadness I couldn't quite capture,
The darkest energy that dimmed my light,
I let you do it to see that you could also be bright.
I threw your bottle in the ocean,
It was made for you, I couldn't keep it.
That would mean keeping part of you without your will,
And I would never do that.

I'll always be the sunlight inviting you to those special
places,
Your face never got to glow in the castle shadows.
You won't come back but if you did, I'd say,
Meet me at the causeway,
For one last chance.
Meet for a dance,
A sweet sun dance.

We will always be what never was and we never knew
what we were trying to be,
Only heaven knows the answer,
That's why I set you free.

For two who never knew the same spaces,
We share this landscape, and when you breathe it I'm
there.
I feel your fingertips on those monoliths,
Tracing back to a life we left,
A life we maybe once had.
The past life of karmic connections need healing.
It's all so revealing, it must mean something.

You're so bad for me and for yourself,
I don't want to dance anymore.
Get away from my stones, you're blocking the sunset

from my eyes.
Listen,
I wish you nothing but good health,
I wish you all the world if it means I get peace of mind,
Knowing you'll never come back again.

My heavy metal lover, with your black jeans on
Those auburn tones in your hair turn me on.
With dazzling eyes you set my heart alight,
Oh lover boy show me what you're made of tonight.
Your explorer on your shoulders,
World in your hands.
You've made many enemies,
But I'm your number one fan.
I am the fire to your water,
Always put on a good show.
But when its all over,
You hold me close to keep my glow.
Oh my Scorpio who'd have known we'd end up like
this,
Me, you and 2am just like it first began.
Your retro lover, with my velvet flares on
Midnight in my hair, I know I turn you on.
Got a smile just for you, hold your hand tight,
Lover girl is taking you home tonight.
The water to my fire,
The steam just keeps rising,
Firm grip pull me closer,
Til the sun meets the horizon.
Oh your Leo loves it when we lay,
Me, you and 2am just like it first began.

To be your muse
In my own insecurity,
Through the lens
You see me differently.
Capturing facets of my being like a hidden stone,
Crashing against the tide of life.
You see the beauty in all I can be,
Even with my insecurity.

The water wants me, I hear her call.
Taking over my dreams and exposing my fears.
I am the sun, I am strong, I will scorn,
Yet here I am, surrounded by water.
Her waves are midnight with diamond clarity,
She's telling me to go home.
The tidal heights are frightening and all those around
me,
See nothing but a calm paradise.
I run, I scream, I run so far
But she's clawing at me,
I threaten my fire and she persists.
She knows I cant swim,
Though ancestrally I can, I live in my fear.
Maybe, I am afraid of how bright I could shine,
But I could never leave him behind.
Torn between my heart and her spell.
Tell the water to leave me,
I am not hers this time,
Let me love, let me be.

Maybe the hips I carry are supposed to reflect the
mountains of my homeland,
And my soft breasts are there to comfort during days of
rain and cold.
My eyes gleam gold when I go back there,
As though they are not mine, and I view the castle in the
same eyes of the old.
Everything before me, is in my body
My feet be flat to walk these hillsides and marshes with
ease.
My courage gifted to me by warriors,
As they fiercely thrust their swords into battle.
The gift of life and blood I shed,
A reminder of magic that led me here to begin with.
And though I fight myself in repeated weeks of pain and
torment,
I remind myself I carry their power.
Perhaps, I am the one healing from battles long ago,
And the only cure for the scars I carry,
Is to return home.

She is bright when I am low, somehow still green under
pure white snow
How can you not love her?
The way her curves carve the skyline every night,
A familiar mother we love without fear,
We run to her when all is lost.
My granny used to say:
'What is for you won't go by you',
And here we are,
Passing each other every day,
Be it in thought or in places amidst hundreds of faces.
We go by, pushing and pulling like a never ending tide.

I can light all the candles and perform every ritual,
I can shout to the ocean and cast every spell,
I can bury my feet in the earth and set fire to the world,
Yet you still have a hold on me.
Years and years and years
Go by.
Go by.
Goodbye.

If the universe needed two lovers to prove it all,
We would be chosen every time.
When you hold me, you ignite my soul,
And repair my broken pieces.
Your love is the intricate tracing of my body,
My fingertips caress you so carefully.
The longing, the desire, the need to be free together,
All whilst being connected as one to achieve ultimate
ecstasy.
You and me, we have it all.
In this superficial world we live in,
We have it all.
Not in bricks and water or ordinary things,
We have it all every moment our souls sing.
It's you, it will always be you,
You are my everything,
And our love is as wide as the universe.

There she goes, my beloved one,
Dancing wild under her sun.
Bringing together everyone,
All but me, she doesn't see me.
I am lurking in the shadows,
Like a waning moon,
Quietly watching her light up the room.
She will never know my heart,
And I will never know her touch.
But just to see her smile,
Is enough.

Also Available from Roswell Publishing

Non-Fiction

An Introduction to Magick – Mozinah the Seer
Phantom Vibrations: A History of Ghost Hunting – BR Williams
Send in the Congregation – Rachael Gilliver
Skin O' Our Teeth – Rachael Gilliver
The Mysterious Wold Newton Triangle – Charles Christian
The Human Element – Rachael Gilliver
You Are Not Broken – Rachael Gilliver

Fiction

Black Ballads – Paul Mackintosh
Letters From Montauk – Rachael Gilliver
Mozinah's Book of Fairy Tales – Mozinah the Seer
The High Price of Fame – Rachael Gilliver

Printed in Great Britain
by Amazon

23407014R00020